A Creature of
Transformation

James Hodgson

Published by Superbia Books
an imprint of
Dog Horn Publishing
45 Monk Ings
Birstall
Batley
WF17 9HU
doghornpublishing.com

This publication and the Young Enigma chapbook competition were supported by a grant from Superbia at Manchester Pride
manchesterpride.com
superbia.org.uk

Writer development, performance workshops and touring funded by Commonword
cultureword.org.uk

Part of Young Enigma,
supporting young and emerging LGBT writers
in the North West of England
youngenigma.com

Edited and designed by Adam Lowe
adam-lowe.com

FALLOUT

Paul wakes up with a heavy head. He doesn't know what to do about it. You would think, as Vice Chancellor, he'd have some solution or a clever fix. He doesn't. Wow. His head is unnaturally heavy. Feels like twenty-tonne heavy. Hydrocephalus. Could be hydrocephalus.

Simon shows him his new shirt.

—Look, Paul, he says. I've got sauce all down the side. Red sauce.

Paul can barely lift his neck. He takes a quick half-look at the stain before reverting to a foetal position.

—So what do you think? says Simon. Simon has an important lunch to go to. He is due to walk the leadership through his excellent plans for consumer disruption.

—Red wine? Ketchup? Do I soak it in pinot grigio? Do we have any left?

Paul says nothing, shrugs, and waves him away.

Simon heads to the kitchen sink. He has become accustomed to the shrug, to solving things himself. He runs the water until the sink is draped in thick sheets of steam. When it looks hot enough he plunges the shirt right in.

—Tits, he says, when the water catches his fingers. Fucking tits!

He rubs his hands to cool them down. Could a shirt melt at boiling point? He stirs the sink with a wooden spoon. He remembers he has to dry his shirt to wear it. Maybe soap will speed things along. Maybe stain remover.

While Simon prepares to spelunk for the Vanish, Paul props his head up with a couple of pillows and tries to settle on exactly what is happening to him. The weight increases every few minutes. Is it a fever? What sort of virus could enflame his poor meningeal fibres so? Virus or no virus it has come at a bad time. A really bad time, in fact, because not only is Paul stewed in panic but he suffers more generally from a profound existential exhaustion, the sort that arises from a long life pushing at basically nothing at all, at emptiness. He tries to roll his head. Nope. For Paul has lately come into full, conscious understanding of something he suspected for a long time: he has never found peace; not with Simon, who he once loved passionately; nor with his career, which is eminent and well-respected but also officious and noxiously dull. Yesterday he got the idea of taking an art class or two, having enjoyed life-drawing as a young man. But it is all too late, especially now, with the head. He can barely move it. He doesn't get to have peace. Peace isn't within his purview. This is a hypothesis the swelling somehow confirms.

Simon is not worried about peace. He is content to delegate the lofty task of peace to those like Paul, or at least until he gets this fucking stain out.

The cupboard is dark. It is also, Simon comes to understand, a geological study of their relationship. They are saving for a trip to Borneo, thus, the products at the front are all from Asda, and all economy. Simon digs back further. A few months before, like a seam of crystal, he finds a four-pack of unopened Waitrose cleaning fluid. Yes, he remembers. He went doolally, high from a promotion, cantering down the supermarket's wide soft-lit aisles like a methamphetamine addict, buying up truffles and a pasta-maker and then later on forcing Paul to eat batch after batch of luxe overstuffed ravioli.

Behind the Waitrose tidemark, which he knows serves as a sort of high point for their coupledom, an emotional climax – sweet Lord Jesus we've actually made it – Simon finds progressively cheaper products: the ladder up which they've clambered. Sink sponges from Sainsbury's (pink middlebrow foam capped in the baize of a pool table). An unused roll of Tesco bin bags, bags that always split apart when loaded no matter how gentle the filling. Robust Poundland rubber gloves, a remnant from when they bought the house and had to eat pot noodles for six months straight. God, Simon flinches at the memory, fully wedged within the cupboard. How hard it was to take a shit.

Finally, after bottles of toilet cleaner fused through time into flint-like outcrops, he starts to find things from the previous occupant or from his mother: ivory-handled brushes the purpose of which is no longer clear; a stethoscope; a crowbar swaddled in grease. And there. He knew he'd seen it. A tin of ancient scouring powder. Ingredients on an international blacklist. Ornate, Victorian embellishments on the lid. So powerful that even in its resting state dust has been repelled an inch away and given the tin a sort of halo. Cockroach carcasses surround it, rearing up as if struck by a terrible revelation before the powder wiped them out. *Mein Gott*, he thinks, when he retrieves the tin. I have become death.

◆

Paul's head swells. He can tell the weight is on the rise because the pillows feel more compressed. What's more troubling is the shape. The shape is on the move in a serious way. There is a new *something* he can feel at the back. This has passed beyond the medical and must, he thinks, be supernatural and/or metaphysical. It must mean something. Only he can't think what. If it is a cosmic joke just because I'm clever, he thinks, then ha ha, very funny, big head, I get it, I get it, I get it.

He wants to shout for Simon. But what's Simon going to do, really? With his skillset Simon could advertise the swelling to death. Simon could radicalise its market position. This isn't Simon's terrain; this is a question of ontology. The feeling in his left ear, the one pinned to the bed, has gone. And is that – what is that? He taps his left cheekbone. A protuberance of some sort. Honestly? It feels like a set of steps. What is going on with his ontology?

◆

Simon pours the powder into the sink. Take that, Beaujolais. The shirt, poor thing, recoils, shivering against the side. Clouds of white acid eat through the water like oncoming nuclear fallout. He hears a clunk from upstairs (Paul has moved his swollen head from the mattress to the floor), and is about to shout to see if everything is okay when the water boils and the shirt begins to give off smoke. Not steam but actual smoke. At which point the doubt creeps in.

◆

Paul has discovered the steps are marble, well-cut, issuing forth from the left side of his face. And there are further additions, too: the steps are flanked on either side by a series of Ionic columns, bookended by stern caryatides. A tablature grows up from his right cheek, filled with tiny cherubs and a crest of some sort, while his ear is dissolved in slanting stone slabs, one after the other, and across his distended forehead pops an acne of windows that cover the new facia in neat rows. Despite his new roof, he can still hear. He can hear Simon swearing.

◆

The sink produces smoke at a crazy rate. Simon runs into the garden and tramples his roses. As the smoke billows up against the kitchen windows it behaves more like paint, blanking everything out, closer to the solid, metallic hydrogen you find at the heart of Saturn (Paul told him this enchanting fact when they were both much younger, and much thinner). Holes appear in the windows. The acrid gas is coming through. It is the ultimate cleaning agent: pale white smoke from beyond the grave. Simon coughs and coughs. He retreats into the street.

—Hi Alison, he says, it's me. Look, I am running late. No, no. Just tell them to hold on a moment. Ten minutes.

He hails a cab. He can pick a new shirt up in town. He settles into the taxi's leather. Not long after, as he leaves the docile suburb for the motorway, all thoughts of the smoke start fading from his mind.

◆

Paul's fate is different. He can feel a library forming in the back of his head – an academic one, with concentric rows of bookshelves stacked with leather-bound books and a team of tiny overqualified librarians that tend to them, sprawling about the lending desks, making herbal teas. An administrative wing flourishes above the library, tiny offices subdividing like cubic bacteria. They better have a centralised HR department, Paul thinks. If not, the battles to set one up will be considerable, fought always in his experience against Faculty HR women with rows of icicles for teeth. Many a sleepless night ahead for the tiny chump who has to steer this ship. Lecture halls and seminar rooms sprout along the top of his cranium. Further buildings blossom off to the side, not in white marble anymore but shoot after shoot of glass. A café, is it? A 'knowledge zone'? He hasn't a clue.

Eventually his doors open. Tens of tiny overpaid professors take up chairs in things like Orchid Botany and French Furniture. Two professors immediately take their sabbatical and try to jet to their second homes along the Côte d'Azur. But this is without success: their planes are, unluckily, swallowed by the white smoke building in the hall. Next, thousands of tiny students approach. How young they seem to him. They complete enrolment. They sit in lectures and take inspiration from Quixote, or don't, or they sext each other on their tiny mobile phones. Tiny administrators pass miniscule paper forms from one office to the next, and back again, laughing at how the academics fill them out. The students rent the flats that have been built in Paul's chest. He watches tiny men meet tiny women in tiny bars, get drunk on tiny quantities of alcohol, stagger back to their tiny flats, and pass out on tiny beds.

What if? he thinks. What if there is an art class somewhere in my head? What if there's an art class, somewhere behind my temple, where a tiny version of me is about to meet a tiny version of Simon? What if it is 1984? A tiny version of Paul unpacks a set of 6B pencils, lending one to his handsome neighbour. And then, thinks Paul, when he sees the tiny Simon sketch a perfect likeness of the model as if he were a natural artist, what if tiny Paul will have the same raw and frightening feeling flood his lungs? He remembers that feeling. The potential held by another is the heart's first object of longing, the purest object of desire. On the basis of this precocious sketch tiny Paul will ask tiny Simon out for a drink. And things will unfold on from there, like they'd opened the map up together.

Paul is suddenly happy and sad at the same time. Happy because he remembers the feelings. How excellent it was to find an artist, a kind, funny artist. How right that sort of destiny seems in the moment's heat. Sad because he knows what was promised therein will in practice release a slow fog, passionless and corrosive, a pale smoke rising up the stairs, even though neither tiny Paul nor tiny Simon could sense it at the time or see it coming. The tragedy is this: when tiny, their hearts are simple, gambolling, a pair of deer in a tiny quiet wood. Their hearts are oblivious to the impending chemical/psychological disaster that will consume them both in the future.

Paul watches the smoke reach the landing. Look how it peels the wallpaper, like it doesn't know how to stop. There must be a solution to it or else what is the point of anything? He is a Vice-Chancellor. It spreads to his bedroom, four or five fingers of white arcing up in grim, neutered rainbows, before it turns its attention to his university. On it comes. It renders the carpet a plain of bubbling plastic. He does not have long left. He knows this. But just before it touches him Paul sucks in a lungful of clean air. It is a punt. In fact the order to his lungs comes in from the gut. One last go, he thinks, summoning the shreds of his courage. In the name of tiny Simon and tiny Paul. He begins to exhale as hard as he can. Everything hangs on a gamble, a last ditch bet, that Paul is a brave man at his base. Brave enough to ask a man out for a drink in '84. And, when faced with the fallout from love, brave enough to try for a life again.

THE MALIGNANT SYMPTOM

When Matthew's mother discovered the lump she froze solid. Matthew expected her to burst into tears, to wail and scream, which she didn't do. Instead she just froze solid. Her fingers locked into a sort of rigor mortis, the joints stiffened, and as a result of this the towels she carried fell to the floor, but otherwise she fell silent and her face drained itself of emotion. To Matthew, who knew exactly what was coming, she resembled the sort of religious statue one might find breaking through the ice-cap of a mountaintop; an impression redoubled by the fact the towels around her feet read easily as snow. The source of the fuss was a lump about as big as a robin's egg growing just below Matthew's solar plexus.

—Cancer, she said. You have a tumour.

—I'm not sure if it is actually a tumour.

—Are there more? Is it AIDS?

—It's not AIDS. Jesus.

—You can't have AIDS, she said. She let out a wail. You just can't! Do you think I like to be the last to know? Your father doesn't know, does he? Have you told him? AIDS, Matthew!

Matthew felt the line of his mother, the outer boundary, move in increments along the hall. Matthew should have known. He had left his bedroom a little early hoping to shower before the house woke up, which was fine, he told himself, totally okay to do that, shower early, no crime. The error (there was always an error) lay in his doing this without a shirt. Yes, a rookie error. And now he would deal the consequences. How familiar life can be, he thought. What a junior mistake. According to the old art of emotional ju-jitsu her outburst should be handled with a shrug. A shrug is the signal for compliance. No, he shrugged. He had not told his father.

—Don't just shrug! We are going to Antigua in June, she said. Your father will be devastated. You'll have to tell him you have cancer right away.

She wiped a few hairs from her forehead and tapped a finger against her open mouth.

—Don't mention AIDS when you tell him. And see if he can rearrange the flights. Antigua, Matthew! I had the strangest dream last night. You were laughing at me. Laughing at your own mother. And I was being blown about by an awful gale, and no matter what I did you wouldn't stop. Isn't that so interesting? And the wind kept on and on like the two were somehow the same thing. Of course now I see it was a vision. I've wanted to go to Antigua for years.

Matthew's mother paced back and forth over the towels.

—Have you told Liza? What does she say about it? I told you not to shrug, Matthew! You must have mentioned something to Liza; wives have a right to know about cancer. I don't expect she was much use. Did she put you in downward dog? Listen to me. I am only saying this because you are going to die, Matthew. Liza is an idiot. Your father thinks that. He doesn't like her, either.

The trip home had been a mistake. Matthew could see that now.

Liza poked her head around the door.

—Is everything okay?

His mother swept her dressing gown up and declared, loudly, that Matthew Has Cancer and Now I Know. It felt to Matthew like a show she'd practiced in front of a mirror, as if she'd been waiting for this day ever since she was a little girl.

Liza maintained a beamy look.

—Carmel, said Liza. Carmel, bless you. It is just a cyst. I have seen hundreds of them. A cyst is impacted skin cells. He's going to the doctor next week, aren't you, wuppy.

—I knew you'd do that, said Matthew's mother. He is going to die and all you want to do is call him wuppy.

—Carmel, said Liza. If you are worried I will lance it now.

—You can't lance cancer.

—I do it all the time at work, said Liza. I did one last month. About this big. There's a trend for filming the lance and putting a video of it online. People get off on the expression of the fluid.

Matthew's mother waved Liza away and went into her bedroom. When she returned she clutched an iPad.

—It is easy to lance, Carmel, said Liza. Do you have a needle? Wuppy, get us a needle, would you? There is one in my suitcase. Front pocket.

Matthew stifled a sigh.

—Last month we had an interesting case, said Liza. Mrs

Cartwright, bless her socks, was convinced a bird would hatch out. The ladies get so imaginative when they come to us. The video of the expression got forty thousand hits.

Matthew's mother, meanwhile, had typed 'cancer' into her iPad. She squinted at the screen.

—Look, Matthew, she said. The internet has lots on cancer. Pictures. Look how big they get. How awful. You and I must go through them all immediately. Not for prognosis, no point for that now, but to be prepared. We need to know what's coming, Matthew. Sit with mummy. If you don't want to read, if you can't bear it, I'll read for you. But first. First I need my varis. Liza! Liza, where are my varies—

Liza toasted the end of a heavy-duty needle with a lighter until it shone white.

—Come here, wuppy.

—What on earth are you doing?

—Nothing to worry about, Carmel. I can lance a bit and leave the rest for the Doctor. What we want to get is some of the expression. Skin cells go into a cheese when impacted.

—Out of the question.

—Carmel. Feel how hard it is. Cancer has a squishiness to it. This is skin cells. Think parmesan.

—I'm his mother.

—Mrs Peterson had a lump like this, except that when they opened it up they found a tiny person.

—Enough, Liza.

—The doctor said it was a twin sister she part-cannibalized in the womb. Somehow it worked its way through her body over the course of her life until one day, in her 80s, it came out on her belly. Tiny feet and hair, all wrapped in a little egg.

—No, said Matthew's mother. She gripped Liza's hand and picked the needle from it, then looked directly into Liza's eyes. You will not lance Matthew.

Matthew could see the concentration on Liza's face. For someone who had been given fair warning, who had heard the tales and knew about the risks, she was coping rather well.

—I wish, said Liza, ah, I wish I could get through to you, Carmel. I understand, ah, how hard it must be.

Matthew's mother hesitated for the second time that morning. She watched Liza's face in just the same way a moray eel would observe a diver, that is, patiently.

—No one ever thinks of you, Carmel.

—No one ever thinks of me.

—Of course, said Liza. You're his mother.

—That's the first sensible thing I think you have ever said. No one thinks about the mother. I have always been there for him. When he went to school I was there – how I gave my life to drive him about – of course no one ever thinks of me – and when I found his dirty magazines, when he wrote such horrible things in his diary – I was always there – and no one ever thinks of me – I just keep calm and carry on – and no one – mothers are treated like the scum of the earth – it's Matthew, Matthew, and never me – he has no idea what I put myself through – and now he's gone and got himself AIDS, cancer, whatever – and I won't complain about it not one – not once! – because that is not the person I am – that's not me – and now he's d-d-dying–

Matthew's mother began to sob, her defences overcome by Liza's inexpert but essentially effective attempt to validate her feelings. Liza took her into a hug, the hint of a grimace tainting her brow. Matthew began to relax.

—There is something you can do, Matthew, said Matthew's mother, directly into Liza's ear. I know a doctor. I know a man you can talk to. He is a therapist. He can prepare you for what comes next. He is a local man. He is very good with death.

Matthew shrugged, locked himself in his old bedroom and lay down on his bed. His mother rapped on the door. He refused to let her in. At first he said he was getting dressed and then he complained of a headache, which added more fuel, as it were, to her particular fire.

♦

The therapist looked at him through circular glasses.

—Tell me about your mother.

Before he could reply, Matthew felt a yawn wash over him. A five a.m. slot was all that could be secured at such late notice.

—I take this yawn to be a parapraxis or a quote unquote defence mechanism articulated against the question of your mother. What are you blocking, is the real question, ha? May I see the symptom?

Matthew lifted up his shirt. The therapist was a man in his fifties who smelt of austere post-war breakfasts: kippers and hard-boiled egg. He looked at the lump and waved his hand.

—A conversion, we call it. I must be honest. I have been given a clear brief, although perhaps your mother credits me with more power than I possess. For example, I cannot, in her words, prepare you for immediate death from cancer. What I can do is this: I can take a symptom such as yours and put forth an understanding more directly related to your situation than so-called hard medicine allows for.

Matthew yawned a third time, almost knocking a small cut glass vase from the side table next to his chair.

—In your case, said the therapist, I can unpack the buried suppressions that have led to your tumour. Indubitably you will find at base a psychic cause—

—So you do think it is a tumour, said Matthew.

—A psychic cause, continued the therapist. We will spend some time today investigating with great care and deliberation. This is why I start with your mother. She related several key facts when she made the appointment: you were a wilful child, even, perhaps, a tearaway; a rowdy embarrassment; and it has only been through great personal sacrifice on her part; through investment in extensive stringency; in rules, that such tendencies have been controlled. Would you agree to her description?

Matthew yawned again.

—Well? Were you a troublesome and naughty child?

—I don't know, said Matthew. Is it important?

—Exceptionally important. She discussed the obsession you held as a child with the question of your own birth. I understand you believed it was impossible for you to have been gestated by your mother. An infantile fantasy, ha? Does this sound familiar? Of course she was under the impression you invented such fantasies – of being swapped out from the cradle, of a mistake at the hospital – to punish her. Do you recognise these feelings? What I suggest is that there is a reason for this acting out that lies in an unconscious belief of some kind, probably about a crime you have committed.

—But you do think it is cancer.

—Whether it is cancer or not is beside the point. What must be resolved today is the cause. Something in your past sits at the root of your illness. Tell me: do you see your mother as an avenging figure, a punishing authority, or do you see her as fragile? Are you her victim or her protector? All little boys go one way or the other, Matthew, and I am certain negative feelings – what in theoretical terms we call aggressive-suppressive libidinal investments – lie at the heart of the tumour's growth.

—Let me get this straight, said Matthew. Your angle is: my mother has given me cancer.

—More properly, the bond itself. The child's response to the maternal imago. There is no blame here – this is therapy – but an incorrect or erroneous response to pure maternal love (a negative response to affection, rather than a positive) could have generated the initial death instinct – or what we call *Todestrieb* – that caused the cancer to grow in the first place.

—It is not her fault, is what you are saying.

—Tell me about Liza. Your mother mentioned she is relatively new in your life. Some months.

—Five and a half.

—Months?

—Years, said Matthew, as he slumped into his chair and stretched out his sad, ape-like arms. We have been married for five and a half years. She knows this.

—Do you think Liza is the right woman for you? I understand she exerts a strong influence on your behaviour, attitudes and ambitions, ha?

Matthew yawned again.

—With an aggressive-suppressive instinct as strong as yours I wouldn't trust your quote unquote gut. In fact if you are to liberate yourself from your death-anxiety you should also liberate yourself from the investments that preserve it: namely, certain specific emotional bonds formed with certain specific other persons. What I am saying is simply, Matthew—

—Liza. Liza has given me cancer.

—In our profession, said the therapist, the correct phraseology would be: she is sustaining or helping to sustain an affective carcinogenesis.

—Because I don't love my mother.

—Crudely put, said the therapist. But not inaccurate.

For the second time in as many days Matthew left the room, this time locking himself in the toilet. The therapist knocked on the door and pointed out that avoidant behaviour was part of the problem. He also tried to talk about Matthew's father. Matthew remained silent, waited out the remaining hour, and, when his time was up, crept quietly out the front door.

♦

—That doesn't sound right, wuppy, said Liza. Why would your mother manipulate the therapist?

Matthew looked at her. He shrugged. Surgery had been planned for early next morning. The cheerful surgeon propounded a cut first ask questions later approach to suspicious tissue growth.

—I work in the healthcare industry and we have standards and regulations in place that stop us doing things like that. Did he use special terminology? Doctors can be intimidating. I think you probably got yourself confused.

Liza arranged the grapes in a bowl.

—You have to get a handle on your negative thinking, wuppy. Perhaps we should do some breathing together. Perhaps we could do a detox. It sounds like your energies aren't very balanced. We could invite Carmel along. She loves to get involved in the things we do. What do you think?

Matthew wasn't listening, for at that very moment a cold sore had broken out on his lump which brought with it a needling sort of pain. The pain, which started as an itch, grew incrementally worse.

—We could get her round to our place, said Liza. We could set it all up for her. Candles, wheat-free thins from M&S. We could do some breathing exercises with her, and make her juices. I think she'd like that. It would make her feel appreciated.

—Liza, get the doctor, said Matthew. The doctor! Christ!

—Wuppy?

Liza was smart. She saw the change, the reddening ulcer, and swore generously. Then she ran to the nurses' station. A few minutes later the paranoid clacks of his mother's heels came down the corridor, followed by the doctor and several nurses, after which the whole lot clustered around Matthew's naked abdomen. The pain, meanwhile, progressed. It became a short, sharp, jabbing pain, concentrated in one particular point on the lump's surface.

—My god, said Matthew's mother, in a tone that she'd lifted straight from a daytime soap. Doctor – you have to do something! Give him morphine, doctor! Put him to sleep! I'll sign the forms – I don't want Matthew in any pain! This is it, my darling boy – be brave! Be strong! Do not go gentle into that good night!

Several nurses tried to pull her from his bed.

—No! said Matthew's mother, clutching handfuls of bedlinen. I will not leave him! Not in his final hour, not me! It is my right! I gave up my life for my child! My right! Don't you take it from me! Don't you dare—

Someone, they later reflected, should have spotted the lump for what it was – an egg.

The shell cracked open. From within came a little bird the same size and shape as a Christmas robin. Eggshell dropped onto the bedsheets. Matthew's mother fainted.

Most fledglings require a month post-egg before they are able to fly. This bird was prepared for flight upon hatching. It shot up above them. The doctor flung his clipboard about in a vain attempt to swat away what shouldn't after all have emerged from a lump on someone's chest. Brown feathers, red belly, black eyes. Unmistakeable.

The bird flew around Matthew. It settled on his head. It took a deep breath in, opening its beak up as wide as possible. With a single powerful exhalation the bird blew the doctor from the room. He zipped along the corridor and hit himself on every set of double doors on the way out. The bird blew Liza through the window. For a minute she held onto its frame but the gust was consistent and powerful, gale force ten, and eventually Liza was sent gently through the air. The wind dropped her off in Rhyll where, a few months later, she opened up a shop that sold wind-chimes and semiprecious stones. Matthew's mother was harder to dislodge. The bird's wild breath blew her against a doorframe to which she clung with crenelated knuckles as white as pack ice, as fierce as the teeth of river rapids. But she would not budge. As she turned her head towards Matthew her cheeks tented with air, no doubt attempting to articulate herself or to pronounce a judgement: you will not win! Luckily enough the bird's exhalations also picked up the cluster of nurses, arms locked to each other for protection, who collided with Matthew's mother and formed briefly into a compound molecule of caring women, professional and amateur, totally stable, that then sailed unharmed through reception, the carpark, the early morning sky, the city's long asphalt rivers, over countryside, the green and open spaces, before touching down near a dairy farm an appropriate distance away.

Matthew was alone. He inspected the shell of his egg and ran a finger over the dent in his skin. It was as if a splinter had worked its way to the surface. The bird hopped off his head and sat on his shoulder. It blinked at him.

Silence fell on the empty ward – though not for long. The bird opened its beak once more. Matthew flinched. In this instance, however, he flinched without cause, for from the bird's tiny throat came a bout of laughter.

Not song, not singing, but laughter. High-pitched, effeminate, human.

RUBIES IN YOUR LEGS

1.

The cook asks the Prince to pick some rosemary for their suppertime dish. The Prince has been fearful of rosemary since childhood. When he bends close to the rosemary bush a man's face appears within it. The face has a beard made of rosemary.

'After something, handsome?' The Prince does not answer. 'Cat got your tongue?' says the face.

The Prince says nothing. After some time the face sighs, takes hold of its beard, and begins to tug. It does itself some real damage to satisfy the Prince's needs. But then so do all of us.

2.

You wake up on a mountainside. The castle at the top is covered in gemstones. When you knock on the door a woman and man answer. They both look like each other.

'You are late,' says the man. 'We have already eaten.'

The woman pulls at the brother's hair, which is long like hers, until small red stones can be seen where you'd expect blood. 'If you are feeling adventurous,' she says 'we could try something else.'

The brother holds out his hand. It might as well be cocaine. 'Go on,' he says. 'Live a little.'

3.

The Prince has sex with a man and then cries into a pillow. The man felt the experience was more or less average but doesn't say anything for fear of offending the Prince. They exchange numbers.

Later, the man holds a barbeque for his colleagues. As he is cooking the burgers he starts to cough. His colleagues supply him with a glass of water. He coughs a ruby into it. A few weeks later he coughs a ruby up when he is giving a speech. The Prince calls him that evening.

'Don't freak out,' he says, 'but I think you should get tested.'

4.

You break into your sister's room. You lock three doors behind you: the outside door, the hallway door, and the bedroom door. You start to copy out her diary into your pocketbook. You get through a full page before you hear someone unlock the outside door.

A cat says to you, 'She already knows you do this, you know.'

You tell the cat to buzz off. You hear someone unlock the hallway door.

'One day,' says the cat. 'You'll just have to come out with it.'

You throw the diary at the cat and it splits down the spine. You try to put the pages back together but it is difficult to mend.

'Confess!' says the cat. 'Confess!'

Meanwhile, someone has reached the bedroom door. Someone is trying the handle.

5.

The Prince tells his sister that he is a bit blue. She makes him a tea with the vine that she dangles from her window. On drinking, the Prince completely trips his balls. Man oh man, the things he sees. When he gets a bit blue again he jumps out of his sister's window. The Prince wakes up in a hospital 21 days later. The nurse says that his leg bones have turned to rubies. He cannot tell if this is because of the tea directly putting rubies in his legs or if he is still tripping balls. Then again, he can't tell if it is not because of the tea (i.e. nothing is related to the trip), or if it all is.

6.

You wake up covered in gemstones. You are so sweaty that you have to peel them off. As you peel them off you grow lighter and lighter. Your sister comes into the room and jumps into the air, planning to land her body next to yours. Time slows down. As you pick each gemstone off she falls slower and slower. It is like Achilles and the tortoise. Your fingers keep finding gemstones to pick off, and your sister keeps slowing.

Jesus, you think. This could go on forever.

7.

You keep a personal ruby in a little gold tube. You take it out when no one is looking and hold it in your mouth. You order a cup of tea from a café. While you wait you watch a blackbird peck at an old man's face. Passers-by try to scare it off.

The waitress brings you the tea. She tuts. The blackbird chops off a part of the old man's ear with its beak which is sharp as flint.

'How unfortunate,' says the waitress.

Privately, you are convinced you have caused the blackbird's attack due to the personal ruby. Your therapist calls this 'magical thinking.'

8.

A pauper exposes himself to you during a public event. You get a good look then order him destroyed by fire. You find the family from whence he came and order them destroyed by fire. You find the village from whence they came and order it destroyed by fire. City after city is put to the torch. Your sister confronts you on the balcony.

'I made you this magical fire-retardant shirt from a pile of dead swans,' she says. 'You'll need it when you burn down the palace.'

The guards take her away.

The last thing she says is: 'Did you hear me, arsehole? You'll need it when you burn yourself alive!'

9.

The Prince catches two men having sex at the side of the road. When he sees them he throws up.

In fact the Prince can't stop being sick, even when there is nothing left in his stomach. The two men try to help. They take him to their flat, find him a blanket and cook him a light supper.

He heaves throughout the night. The two men hush him and mop his brow. Each time he heaves it is worse, until at four a.m. he heaves so strongly he throws himself inside out. All the way.

With his surfaces reversed, he calls himself 'the Princess'. He finds work in a nightclub downtown and does Tuesdays and Fridays. He's pretty good.

METAMORFOSIS

Following the revelation, a number of things changed.

Sex, for one, which had become meaningless. David registered this in an almost instinctual way, in the gut. Desire evaporated.

Of course he needed proof. The same day he felt this evaporation he found and hooked up with some nameless soul, some guy, and when he cleared off and David stood in front of the open window and waited for the microwave ping in his inner core (which was a sign from the dark internal gremlin that *yes*, aha, that has hit the spot) nothing came – nothing; not a sign, not a lick of relief. The Mexican city moved beneath his feet. Sex had been transformed. And the revelation, its dumb consequence, remained with him.

He exhaled for 20 minutes, maybe an afternoon. He had an article to write. He had pitched to *Inveterate World* on a character called Malintzin. Malintzin was an Aztec princess who slept with Hernan Cortez, the original conquistador, and taught him to speak Nahuatl. This might not have seemed a big deal but Cortez used his Nahuatl to dominate the Aztecs, ushering in a new age of what could justifiably be seen by the Aztec people as pure and total hell – slaughter, plague, etc. A bartender, a handsome Oaxacan, had told David an extra, fruity twist: in return for access to her people, Malintzin gave Cortez a nasty bout of syphilis – the first case for a Spaniard – and somehow also passed on syphilis to his sons; and then went on – how, who knows – to spread syphilis all about the Iberian peninsula; so watch out, Spaniards, for hell shall be revisited on your best and brightest for Cortez's initial diabolical deal – the moral of which seemed to be *be careful what you wish for.*

David wiped another man's sweat from his chest.

Outside, the town roared through its evening like a beehive gathers itself for a downpour, bars stacking and unstacking their plastic chairs, drinkers testing the mad dust for rain. Cries sent into the air. The buildings in this city were all unfinished. David could feel the sweat on his back, as if he'd just emerged from a dirty river.

What's that? He looked into the mirror. It could be shadow. Did the guy notice? A patch of skin, very dark in comparison, in fact as dark as a crocodile's. David lifted his right arm up. He could feel the sweat pool down the cleft at the foot of his spine, the arrowhead. He lifted his left arm. There. Another patch, just underneath the armpit. Dark skin growing there. Unheeded. Dark green skin.

◆

Whereas in London the men required many boxes to be ticked before dispensing their love, in Peru, for example, the men were easy; and in Brazil, and in Mexico and Columbia, they were also easy; and they were easy in Chile and easy in Panama, also. David did not keep a serious job. He did not have a serious life. He pitched to *Inveterate World* under the moniker Horny Goatweed about the differences in cruising habits across the Americas. He pitched on travellers' cocks and he pitched on the etiquette of rimming. The site took him on because everything is permitted at *Inveterate World*. He pitched and had sex and pitched again – the site first requiring a pitch and then, yes, actual content either unconventional or culturally enriching – and he having working up to paid contributor knew more or less how to do both. So then he knew how to receive monies to live on and rent private rooms and move from place to place, and be with easy men who demanded very little from him. He had a good angle on Malintzin. So she let the Spanish in. Was she really a bad person? He had a sweet title for the piece. You Won't Believe Why the Aztecs Hated on This One Woman.

His parents were initially supportive – Live your life! You do you! – but in practice, over time, they had engineered from him a quiet withdrawal. Soft Brexit. You are still our son, but why can't you be like your broth—, and who are all these Josés and Diegos you so shamelessly talk about—, we're not stupid—, and we forgot to say about coming for Christmas, perhaps next year—, you're thirty four next year—, and we forgot to say your brother now has a kid—

You Won't Believe Why His Parents Are Hating on This One Liberal Guy.

David looked out of the window, listening to the dark internal gremlin; running his fingers over his clavicles, his shoulder. He made himself a coffee but couldn't drink it. He watched Mexico hurry and roar, homes flicking their lights up into the evening squall. He made a sandwich but his fingers trembled and he covered his tiny desk in crumbs.

Perhaps it was the specific man. He knew it wasn't, deep in the gut, but the promise somehow teased him: perhaps he could go back in time, pre-revelation; pre-moment of truth. He showered and lay on his bed. Perhaps he needed a different type. He sniffed his armpit like a chimp would when watched in a zoo, with shame. He caught sight of the dark green patch on his flank. He could not work. He dressed. He went to a bar.

◆

Most of the gringo bars followed a familiar pattern. Barman in orange knit, kitchen where cocaine is done, spider plants held in colourful crocheted holders, odour of hash and tequila, Americans.

One American caught his eye. He was familiar, but only from the questions David could read in his face: do I shed my past and become a new man here in Latin America? Perhaps through the transformative power of experience x – where x is anything referred to as medicine, including peyote, san pedro, and perhaps even this blunt I am being offered by this very friendly barman? David could read these questions like a nursery rhyme. Mexico was a holy land for Americans. David tapped the American on his shoulder.

—Hello.

—Hi, in return, spoken in capitals. HI.

David had it spot on. The American was a spring-breaker, here to escape the impending tombstone of a life at Meryl Lynch. His eyes were somewhat too close together but his jaw was good and his arms were thick and he was easily impressed.

You ever hear about the pineal gland as a direct map of energy centres onto the body? said David. A scientific basis in quantum theory. Connective tissue. Biology. What do you think consciousness is, said David, and then, a little later, Have you tried anything stronger? and finally do you want to come back to mine?

◆

—You know I'm not gay specifically.

David sat him on the side of the bed.

—Gay doesn't exist, said David. We are made of nameless energetic impulses.

When David kissed him the American gave in. He could taste a brief but precise history: first the blunt, then tequila, both smoke and booze framed with toothpaste, and then after that the earthy taste that defines a man's baseline, the code behind the drama. David took off the American's shirt. His body was long and his armpits full. For a moment David through the magic had somehow returned – look at this man who is willing! – and on that basis he unzipped his own fly.

Yes, the American was eager. He was also totally clueless and his moans were put on and distressing. He wanted the show, the activity of transformation. David found himself rolling his eyes. The moans continued. The American took a hand over the mouth as encouragement. When David started to wilt he tried to explain that with guys you didn't always have to stay hard, one could serve the other's pleasure, but the American grew embarrassed and came frantically about a minute later.

—Sorry, said the American.

—Don't be sorry, said David.

—I had fun. Did you have fun?

—I wish you'd kept quiet. There are French people next door.

—Man, it was good. It was, like, hot. Did you find it hot?

—Of course.

—But you didn't finish off. I had fun though.

Silence.

—That's why I finished off so quick, said the American. Did you find it hot?

—Not really.

—Was it me?

—No, he said. I am going through something.

—You know what? I feel like we know each other. You can tell me.

David looked again.

—We could go again, said the American. If you want to. I can cancel the bus ticket. I was supposed to be going to Oaxaca but I can cancel if you want to try again tomorrow morning?

—I have lost interest in sex, said David. The thing I am going through. As a consequence of something else, something I did.

24

—What did you do?

—It wouldn't make sense to you.

—Man, I just sucked your cock.

—I don't think you'd understand.

The American had a long back and long mousey hair. He had the body of a man that had been unquestioningly drilled by a drill sergeant. The American swung his legs over the side of the bed and held his head in his hands. He went to the toilet. When he came back he posed sideways in the doorframe.

—Is it my fault? You don't have to tell me if it's my fault.

—It is something I am going through.

The American leafed through David's Spanish dictionary.

—Alright, said David, surprising himself. I'll tell you. I found out why I have sex.

—Why?

—I found out why I have sex. I took this drug. Medicine.

—Peyote?

—Something like that. I found out exactly *why*.

—And now you can't do it. Isn't it, like fear of women? Of pussy.

—It certainly isn't fear of pussy.

—We know why we have sex. Making babies.

—I couldn't give two shits about making babies.

—You can tell me.

—It doesn't matter. I found out. Once you've seen the rope in the room – have you heard that story?

—I don't think so.

—A man is in a dark room. He sees a snake in the corner, which makes him scared. Then someone shines a light on the snake and shows it up to be a piece of coiled rope, and so even if the room is dark again he'll always know the rope for what it is. The whole thing is about fear.

—Can't you get a pill or something? Or see a shrink?

David shrugged and turned to the window.

A shrink would say, *Oh yah, zis is very typical.*

The Mexican sky was violet and starless.

—What is that?

The American pointed at the patch of dark green on his shoulder.

—A birthmark.

His mother, shaking a letter at him. The letter explains that due to inappropriate behaviour with a pupil in the year below they are very sorry but will need to expel David from this and all future terms. His father sits in an armchair, crossing his legs at the ankle. You were supposed to go to Oxbridge, says his mother. She makes the second 's' of 'supposed' into a long hiss.

—I mean that, said the American.

On David's other shoulder (he had not noticed this till now) was a further patch of dark skin, and at the crest of the patch grew a nodule. David touched it.

—Are you sick, said the American.

—Have you heard of Malintzin? said David. Sometimes she gets called *La Malinche*. She's to do with Hernan Cortez, the conquistador. Do you know Hernan Cortez?

The American started to dress. His fingers stumbled on the stiff jean buttons of his fly.

—What is it? he said. Are you full blown? Jesus, do I need to get tested?

David held his arms to his chest.

—Am I going to die? I'm not gay. I can't die.

—There is no cure for what you have.

—Jesus Christ.

—That was cruel, said David. I am sorry. Do you forgive me?

The American did not respond until his polo shirt had been pulled over his neck. His hair was trapped in a sheen of new sweat that broke across his forehead.

—Asshole, said the American. Jesus Christ. It's all over you.

He threw his hands up and left.

When David was alone again he returned to the mirror. The dark skin had spread quite rapidly. It spread around his shoulderblades. No wonder the American had said something. A nodule grew on the crest of his shoulder. Two, actually. Small enough. At the tip of one nodule you could make out the beginnings of something white.

He sat down at his desk. He had one last shot at things. He said this to himself. One last go at the article. If he could just write it and get published in *Inveterate World* perhaps somehow there was still a place for him. He knew, deep down, the logic was off. It was a fool's effort. But the Mexican evening felt long and open, full of hope, and the mix of sweat on his back had become a cold uncomfortable lace, one that pooled along his spine and ran down intermittently into the small of his back, then to the plastic chair, where it pooled again, and he found he could not think straight. Is this, he wondered, all part of the change?

David began to type.

♦

A couple of months before he slept with the American, David had visited a town in Peru so high up in the Andes he'd needed to lie still for three days upon arrival. The men there were nervous but easy. Although it was expensive to rent out private rooms night after night, David took the joy he wanted all the same, flush with money from *Inveterate World*. He felt totally free of shame.

A barman named Papa Tio offered to show him dancing cacti for three hundred *soles*. David was here to experience and write about the real wow events. He was here to investigate reality beyond the normative social machine. Dancing cacti ticked the boxes. He could write for *Inveterate World* on dancing cacti.

Later that day they hiked up to the top of the valley, and beyond that, onto the scrub, during which time Papa Tio told David all about the cactus-people, and David took notes. The cactus-people were spirits from the underworld that danced at the start of the evening. They took human form and preserved the knowledge of the quechua people, the *runakuna*. There was science behind the dancing, said Papa Tio. San Pedro, which is a medicine, you take this, and then you affect quantum theory. David didn't think so. Perhaps he'd write an expose. You Won't Believe What This One Guy Uses Quantum Theory to Explain.

After eight hours' hike beyond the town they stopped. The landscape was brown, hilly, plantless, trees starved off by solar radiation and thin almost acidic air. Mountain in one unbroken flank, a rejecting wall. Papa Tio called the sun 'raw yang'. He gave David a flask of liquid.

—Drink this, said Papa Tio, pointing to a group of cacti. It is medicine. It will make them dance.

—Are they actually going to dance? What is it?

—Just do as I say.

The taste was bitter. Papa Tio read a newspaper. About half an hour later David threw up. Then after some more time, harder to measure, the cacti in the middle distance, a group of five or six, began to move. They were the cacti you'd expect, the kind you've seen in Westerns – tall, spiny, with dark green limbs festooned at the tips with white flowers. The shift was hard to track. A cactus first, and then a person. The evening light turned oblongs and triangles of prickled cactus flesh into five o'clock shadow, the shoulder-pads of gladiators. Let's be specific: they began to resemble men.

After about an hour of dancing, David worked it out.

—They are not dancing. *No bailan*, he said.

Papa Tio told him to be quiet and returned to his newspaper.

—That is not dance, said David.

He knew what to do. He had never been more certain. He stood up, confidence tearing like a wasp through his arteries. He walked towards the cactus-men. He began to unbutton his shirt. How hard the sunlight on his skin, even in the evening. A few hours of exposure would transform it into a tawny brown. He kicked off his boots. He unpicked his socks.

—Hey, shouted Papa Tio, part in English and part in Spanish. Hey! Hey! Get back here!

He could see six cactus-men. Fucking, not dancing.

—Hey, gringo! Put your goddam clothes back on!

Yes, he was going to do it alright.

He didn't know where to begin. Then, he did.

—Ah, Jesus Christ. *Maricón!*

This was it. The true jazz of life. David looked back. He had worked it out. He let it happen, arching his back, staring Papa Tio in the eye. Here comes the wow event. Here comes the p-o-i-n-t.

—*Maricón!* Have you no fucking shame?

David was close to the wow. Real close. He could taste it, this thing that would resolve the picture. It grew like a bulb within his gut. But right when it was due to pop, when he was owed the deep true message, the point, oh god—

—pfft. A stupid pfft. He looked up. The starlight, weak and old. Ice on his breath. Nothing. Nada. Zip. When he looked back Papa Tio's face was a total blank too. Papa Tio, who had run after him some way then stopped, bemused, perplexed, or in fact just totally blank. Papa Tio's face gave him nothing. The air was close to pure void. His breath was white. And there was a deathly silence. Is that right, he thought. That can't be right. The grave of starlight. David looked right into Papa Tio's face. His face held the truth like a fist. What a clown. What a desperate effort to piss off his parents. Just a dumb kid. A shrink would say, *Oh yah, zis is very typical.* A kid who runs straight for the shock factor, the main event. Fuck you, mother. A kid who stumbles upon a lot of pure dull emptiness.

♦

He finished the Malintzin article the day after he slept with the American.

That night he got drunk on his own and wandered around the cool Mexican streets. He spoke to nobody. In the morning, a little hungover, he checked for typos and sent the article on to *Inveterate World.* He concluded on the side of Cortez, in a way, who was simply looking for the next big thing when he seduced Malintzin. Perhaps he even wanted to get syphilis. Perhaps he slept around. Perhaps he was sick of being Hernan Cortez. Just totally sick of himself.

He waited.

The editor made many corrections. First, David had missed the accents on Hern*án* Cort*és*. But essentially the thesis was wrong, and the idea that syphilis was transmitted via or as a result of the conquest of the Aztec peoples was offensive, and if David was going down this road then he should remedy the outright cultural insensitivity and clear exhibition of privilege by registering the singular importance of this woman, Malintzin, not some straightforward floosy but mother to a people who have already had enough problematic neo-imperialist journalism done about them, thank you very much, and did not need any more.

—Jesus, said his editor. Syphilis? Cortés? Stick to rimjobs and watersports, David. Go fuck a celebrity. What have you been smoking?

So that's how David knew he was finished with *Inveterate World,* and that his life as he had lived it up to that point was over. No more Horny Goatweed. It was a sign, a message, a burning bush, and David could read it now. For the first time he could read it.

He prevaricated a couple of days, then took a flight plus a very long bus back to Huaraz, the town high up in the Andes. He recognised the people. Peruvian *campesino* women in bowler hats and bright pink, orange or green skirts. He stopped off at a hostel but did not talk to anyone. He wore a dark long-sleeved shirt and long trousers. He thought he saw the American in the crowds and turned onto another street. He was overcharged for a pack of cigarettes which he didn't smoke. He got lost, or he pretended to get lost.

Really he was just putting things off. When he cut the bullshit out he tied his hiking boots tight and trekked to the top of the *cordillera blanca*, trekked through past wild horses and dwindling glaciers until he hit the broad low hillocks of the uppermost part of the Huancayo valley. To the uninitiated this terrain seemed to be a desert, carved up at its edges by low walls of glassy rock – grey-brown soil, plantless except for tightly-clustered cacti – but it was hemmed by the cordillera's rejecting mountains a half-mile away, which gave it the sense of being a starter platform for some roaring majesty still further off again.

He found a good spot. He dug a bowl in the dry soil and peeled away his clothes, the dark-green having spread down across his whole body, and he planted his feet into the bowl and sat in lotus modified to accommodate the angle of his legs. Then he waited. He looked directly up at the white ball of unfiltered sun, raw yang, and waited.

He did not send word to his parents. They were not receiving. How dumb he'd been to think any different. They had never received, not once, and they never would.

He waited for the nodules that now covered his shoulders to open. He waited for the flowers that lay inside to offer themselves up to the sun. And the buds would open, in time. And the flowers would offer themselves to the sun's raw yang without a second thought, as wild and shameless as they were.

AUTHOR'S ACKNOWLEDGEMENTS

I would like to thank A. for his undying love. I match it with unending gratitude. 'The Malignant Symptom' and 'Metamorfosis' are unpublished. A previous version of 'Fallout' has appeared at *Queen Mob's Teahouse*. A previous version of 'Rubies in your legs' has appeared at *Ellipsis Zine*.

About Superbia Books

This book was one of three winners of the Superbia Chapbook Competition. The prize was funded by Manchester Pride, and the three winning entries comprise the debut publications under the Superbia Books imprint of Dog Horn Publishing. All three chapbooks will be launched as part of Manchester Pride's Superbia strand of arts and cultural events in Greater Manchester.

Additional funding was provided by Commonword in order to mentor the writers, prepare them for publication and organise launch events. Commonword is the literature development agency for the North West.

The editing and mentoring was undertaken by Adam Lowe on behalf of Young Enigma. Founded with seed money from Commonword, Young Enigma supports young and emerging writers from Manchester and the North West.

Find out more at superbia.org.uk, cultureword.org.uk and youngenigma.com.

Superbia Chapbook Winners

A Creature of Transformation, James Hodgson
Strain, Kenya Sterling
Vivat Regina, Maz Hedgehog

ND - #0183 - 270225 - C0 - 229/152/2 - PB - 9781907133831 - Matt Lamination